Abyssinian Cats

BY TAMMY GAGNE

The Child's World®

Published by The Child's World®
1980 Lookout Drive • Mankato, MN 56003-1705
800-599-READ • www.childsworld.com

Acknowledgments
The Child's World®: Mary Berendes, Publishing Director
Red Line Editorial: Editorial direction
The Design Lab: Design
Amnet: Production
Design elements: iStockphoto; Brooke Becker/Shutterstock
Images; Shutterstock Images; Willem Havenaar/Shutterstock
Images

Photographs ©: iStockphoto, cover, 1, 5, 10, 14, 17, 23;
Brooke Becker/Shutterstock Images, cover, 1; Shutterstock
Images, cover, 1, 9, 13, 19; Willem Havenaar/Shutterstock
Images, cover, 1; Andre Nantel/Shutterstock Images, 7;
Fuse/Thinkstock, 21

Copyright © 2015 by The Child's World®
All rights reserved. No part of this book may be reproduced or
utilized in any form or by any means without written permission
from the publisher.

ISBN 9781626873858
LCCN 2014930612

Printed in the United States of America
Mankato, MN
July, 2014
PA02226

ABOUT THE AUTHOR

Tammy Gagne has written dozens of books about the health and behavior of animals for both adults and children. Her most recent titles include Great Predators: Crocodiles *and* Super Smart Animals: Dolphins. *She lives in northern New England with her husband, son, and a menagerie of pets.*

CONTENTS

Wild Thing

Abyssinians are a popular cat **breed**. It's easy to see why! These smart and friendly cats are fun. They have a lot of energy and love to play. Abyssinians are perfect pets for people with plenty of energy.

The Abyssinian looks like it came from the jungle. It reminds many people of the Egyptian wildcat. Abyssinians came from this larger cat.

Today there are around 600 million house cats in the world. Cats in the United States belong to one of 42 different breeds. Many people call this breed "Aby" for short.

Abys are tabby cats. This means they have light coats with dark stripes. Their short hair is easy to **groom**.

Abys like kids, but they don't like to be held. Abyssinians want to be moving all the time.

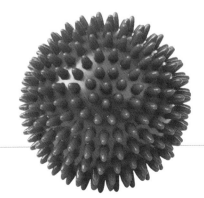

Abyssinians look similar to their African ancestors.

Out of Africa – or Asia?

Abys are believed to be one of the oldest cat breeds in the world. They look like cats in ancient Egyptian art.

Because of its name, many people think the breed came from Abyssinia. This was the old name for Ethiopia. Research shows the breed started in Southeast Asia. Scientists learned this by studying Abyssinian's genes.

The breed's name may come from a story in Great Britain. British soldiers came home from the Abyssinian War in 1868. One soldier brought a cat back with him. This cat was then bred with a British shorthair. Some people think the kittens were the first Abyssinians. No one knows if the story is true.

The cat the British solider brought home was named Zula.

The Abyssinian breed dates back thousands of years ago.
Abys look like those cats seen in Egyptian art.

Surviving the Wars

Abyssinian cats likely existed long before 1868. Many people think the breed came to Europe from India. Merchants and other travelers could have brought the cats to Great Britain.

Great Britain recognized the Abyssinian as a breed in 1882. The breed did not move to the United States right away. Abys arrived 20 years later in the early 1900s. The breed soon became very popular.

Abyssinians first appeared in U.S. professional cat shows in 1909. More people began to want an Aby. Americans began breeding them by the 1930s.

There were two world wars in the 1900s. This made it hard for British cat **breeders**. They could not keep

The end of World War II left only about 12 Abyssinians in England.

the breed going. The United States and Holland were able to help.
They sent cats to breeders in England. The parents of these cats came
from Great Britain years earlier.

Abys became the popular new breed in the United States in the 1900s.

Look at Those Ears!

The first thing many people notice is an Abyssinian's large ears. They are shaped like triangles. The ears bend forward near the tops. The cats look like they are always paying attention.

Abyssinians have big eyes. The iris may be gold or deep green. The iris is surrounded by a darker color. Their eyes curve up at the corners. They look as if they are wearing eye makeup like that worn by the Egyptian queen Cleopatra.

The Abyssinian's body is of medium length. It is athletic with long legs. They have oval-shaped feet. This makes it look like they are standing on their tiptoes. They have long tails. The tail is thinnest near the tip.

Abys are much smaller than Egyptian wildcats. Most Abyssinians weigh between 6 and 10 pounds (2 and 4 kg). Females are on the smaller side.

The ears and the eyes are two of the first features people notice about Abyssinian cats.

A Range of Color

An Abyssinian's fur adds to its different look. They have a tabby **ticked** coat. This means the fur is lighter near the skin. It is darker toward the tips. Four to six colors are found on each hair **shaft**. The different colors mix together.

Abyssinians come in many colors. These include blue, fawn, ruddy, and red. Ruddy-colored is the most common. These cats have a tan coat with many colors of reddish-brown.

All Abyssinians have cream-colored hair around their noses. It is also around their lips and chins. The hair around their eyes is also lighter.

Abys come in many different colors. Red is a common coat color.

Playful Personality

The word most people use to describe the Abyssinian is active. These cats are always on the move. They are known for acting silly.

The breed is also known for its smarts. Abys are always exploring their surroundings. They like to climb. You may find your Aby on top of the tallest furniture. They like to be where they can see everything.

Abyssinians have excellent skills. They move gracefully even in the highest places. They usually don't knock things off shelves.

The playful breed is jokingly called the Aby-silly-an.

Abys are always moving around. It is common to see them climbing inside and outside.

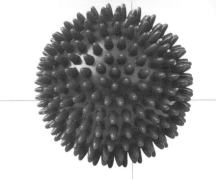

Not Your Typical Cat

Abyssinians usually like all people. They love their family members. They also warm up to strangers quickly. Many Abys get along well with dogs, too. They do not like sharing attention, though. Most Abyssinians want to be the only cat in the house.

Most cats do not like water. But Abyssinians do! Give your Aby a large water bowl. But be warned! You may find your cat splashing around in the dish.

Abyssinians can be taught to walk on a leash. It is easy to teach them tricks. Many Abys teach their owners a trick or two. This breed is good at getting people to do what it wants.

Abyssinians enjoy playing in water. They may even drink out of a faucet!

Keeping an Aby Entertained

Life with an Abyssinian is never boring. These cats want to be with their owners as much as possible. It's important to spend time with Abys. They will get into trouble if alone for too long. You may come home to a big mess. Abys are good at unwinding entire rolls of toilet paper. Toys can help stop this.

Abyssinians love to chase things. Lighted balls and beams from laser pointers are favorites. Noisy toys can also hold their interest. A scratching post may help stop an Abyssinian from using its claws on furniture.

Abyssinians do best in larger homes. Apartments can be too small for their adventurous spirits. They are good indoor cats. But they like to see outside. A bird feeder can provide hours of entertainment. Abys are very curious.

Some Abyssinians have been known to open kitchen cupboards.

It is important to keep Abys busy throughout the day. Scratching posts stop Abys from ruining furniture.

Daily Care

It is easy to take care of an Abyssinian. There are simple steps. Take your cat to a **veterinarian** yearly. A vet can tell if your cat is sick. They will treat it to help it get well.

Abyssinians are usually healthy cats. But some have health problems. One problem can be with their knees. Sometimes the cat's knee pops out of its **socket**. This hurts and makes it hard for the cat to walk.

Many Abyssinians may also have gum problems. Brushing your cat's teeth weekly is a good idea. You could even brush them every day!

Abyssinians do not shed much. But you will need to brush your cat. This should happen once a week. Brushing removes dead hair. It also makes their fur look shiny.

Abyssinians do not need many baths. Owners need to bathe them only if they are dirty.

Abyssinians can live between 12 and 15 years. It is important to take good care of them. Spending time playing with Abys will also help them have long happy lives.

Abys will help keep themselves clean by licking their paws.

Glossary

breed (BREED) A breed is a group of animals that are different from related members of its species. Abyssinians are one cat breed.

breeders (BREED-uhrs) A breeder is a person that breeds a specific group of animals. British cat breeders had trouble breeding Abyssinians during the two world wars.

genes (JEENS) Genes are the parts of cells that control the appearance and growth of a living thing. Scientists studied Abyssinians' genes to learn where they came from.

groom (GROOM) To groom is to clean and keep up the appearance. It is important to groom your cat's coat.

iris (EYE-riss) The iris is the colored portion of the eye. Abyssinian cats can have gold or green irises.

research (REE-surch) Research is collecting information about a subject. Research shows Abyssinian cats came from Southeast Asia.

shaft (SHAFT) The shaft is the part of the hair that can be seen. Abyssinians have four to six colors on each shaft.

socket (SOK-it) A socket is an opening that holds something. Some Abyssinians' knees pop out of their sockets.

ticked (TIK-ed) Ticked is when there is a lighter color closer to the body. Abyssinians are ticked tabby cats.

veterinarian (vet-ur-uh-NER-ee-uhn) A veterinarian is a doctor who treats animals. It is important to take your cats to the veterinarian.

To Learn More

BOOKS

Bailey, Gwen. *What Is My Cat Thinking?*
San Diego: Thunder Bay Press, 2010.

Gagne, Tammy. *Amazing Cat Facts and Trivia.*
New York: Chartwell Books, Inc., 2011.

WEB SITES

Visit our Web site for links about Abyssinian cats:
www.childsworld.com/links

Note to Parents, Teachers, and Librarians: We routinely verify our Web links to make sure they are safe and active sites. So encourage your readers to check them out!

Index